First published in the United States, Great Britain, Canada,
Australia, and New Zealand in 1999 by North-South Books,
an imprint of Nord-Süd Verlag AG, Gossau Zürich, Switzerland.
First paperback edition published in 2002 by North-South Books.

Distributed in the United States by North-South Books Inc., New York.

Library of Congress Cataloging-in-Publication Data

Falda, Dominique.
[Schatzkiste für Freunde. English]
The treasure chest / by Dominique Falda; translated by Rosemary Lanning.
p. cm.
Summary: Squirrel digs up a treasure chest and all the other animals fear
he will forget them when the buried treasure makes him rich.
[1. Buried treasure—Fiction. 2. Squirrels—Fiction. 3. Animals—Fiction.
4. Friendship—Fiction.] I. Lanning, Rosemary. II. Title.
PZ7.F1885Tr 1999   [E]—dc21 98-42105

A CIP catalogue record for this book is available from The British Library.

ISBN 0-7358-1049-4 (trade edition) 10 9 8 7 6 5 4 3 2
ISBN 0-7358-1050-8 (library edition) 10 9 8 7 6 5 4 3 2 1
ISBN 0-7358-1696-4 (paperback edition) 10 9 8 7 6 5 4 3 2 1
Printed in Belgium

For more information about our books, and the authors and artists who
create them, visit our web site: www.northsouth.com

The Treasure Chest

Dominique Falda

Translated by Rosemary Lanning

North-South Books / New York / London

One night Squirrel could not sleep.
He was hungry, so he jumped down from
his tree and began to dig.

He thought he would find a hoard of nuts he had buried long ago.
Instead, he found a treasure chest!

Owl, who never slept at night,
saw what Squirrel had found.

She flew over the forest, hooting: "Treasure! Squirrel has found buried treasure!"
But no one heard. Everyone else was fast asleep.

When the sun rose, Owl's friends woke up at last.

"Have you heard?" she hooted. "Squirrel dug up a treasure chest last night!"

"What was in it?" asked Mole.

"Yes, tell us what was in the chest!" cried Rabbit, Badger, and Bear.

"Wait! Let me guess," said Rabbit.
"I think it was carrots. Lots and lots
of carrots. I could have six every day."

"No," said Badger. "I think the chest was full of balloons. I would love to have some balloons to play with."

"Don't be silly," said Bear. "The chest
was full of honey. Sweet, golden honey."

"I hope there was a pair of glasses in that chest," said Mole. "Then I could see more clearly."

Owl clucked impatiently. "Don't be silly," she said. "Treasure chests are always filled with gold and silver, pearls, diamonds, and other precious stones."

"And you mark my words," said Owl. "Now that Squirrel has found this treasure he will buy the whole forest and drive us all away."

"Drive us away?" gasped the animals, horrified.
"Squirrel is our friend," said Rabbit.
"When someone gets rich," said Owl, "he forgets his friends, and thinks only of himself."

"I don't believe it!" cried Mole.
"Come on, let's find Squirrel."
And off they ran.

"What was in the treasure chest, Squirrel?" asked
the animals anxiously.

"Why are you so worried?" asked Squirrel. "There is
always something nice in a treasure chest."

"So you're rich now," said Rabbit.

"Well," said Squirrel, "I do have a chest full of seeds,
nuts, and honey."

"Seeds, nuts, and honey?" echoed the animals.

"That's right," said Squirrel, smiling broadly.
"And I've made them into a wonderful cake
for all of us to share."

"We thought you were rich," said Owl sheepishly.
"Well, I *am* rich," said Squirrel. "But only because
I have all of you for friends."